Vitas Luckus

The Hard Way

'In spite of everything, in spite of the fact that there were dark clouds, horrifying clouds, if you were to sug-
gest that we led a tragic life I would react by saying that we didn't. It was the most beautiful and buoyant, the
most joyful life you can imagine. The world has never seen a happier woman than I was at the time.'

Jelena Sergejevna Bulgakova, **on the death of her husband, the writer** Michail Bulgakov.
After the death of Vitas Luckus, **his widow** Tanya Luckiene **came across this passage in a magazine.**

Vitas Luckus

The Hard Way

Photographer, Lithuania 1943-1987

EDITION STEMMLE

The photographic work is based on and compiled of the handmade
books Vitas Luckus made.

Text copyright by the authors
Authors: Laima Skeiviene, Herman Hoeneveld, under the auspices
of Tanya Luckiene
Translation: Martin Rometsch
Editing: Martin Rometsch, Peter J. Grimshaw
Design: Cees de Jong and Jan Johan ter Poorten, V+K Design,
Naarden, The Netherlands
Photolithography: Repro Fuchs GmbH, Salzburg, Austria
Printing and binding: Passavia Druckerei GmbH, Passau, Germany
ISBN 3-905514-13-3

Contents

If it were not for the rebellious spirit of Vitas Luckus, Lithuanian photography as a whole over the last two decades would seem exaggeratedly harmonious. His many-sided talent has left its impact on virtually every field of photography: documentary, portrait, surrealist and advertising photography alike.

For a long time many of Luckus' discoveries and innovations were denied to us since he was a 'prohibited' photographer. It was very difficult to organize exhibitions or publish his work, and only with the help of his many Muscovite friends was he able to hold exhibitions in Moscow and Tallin in 1982. In Lithuania only two events were organized during his entire artistic career: a small exhibition in the Vilnius Artists' House in 1985, and a fragmentary review of his works in the Vilnius Photography Gallery one year later. His first foreign publication in the Czech magazine 'Photography Review' resulted in an extraordinary scandal – the entire Russian edition was confiscated. Following this, nobody dared publish his work for many years.

The problems experienced by Luckus with publicity are due to his contempt for conventional interpretations of reality. Photography was subject to much more rigorous ideological supervision than music or painting – and he refused to stick to traditional standards of beauty. While all the 'non-beautiful' aspects of painting can be attributed, at least in theory, to the artist's imagination, photography can become a document of social reality at any time. Luckus used to rebel regularly against the dated social conventionality of photographers in his day – usually due to self-censorship or natural adjustment – but the obedience of young photographers to artistic conventions he considered even more dangerous.

Vitas Luckus' most important work comprises his photographic documentations of the Central Asian republics, the Caucasus, Estonia and Bashkiria. They have revealed him as a reformer of traditional romantic realism (together with Aleksandras Macijauskas), and an unrivalled master of composition.
He was the first to make a decisive move against the confinement of Lithuanian photographers, and to add pictures from the outside world to the traditional range of national topics. Since his reports go far deeper than

Burning Desire

Laima Skeiviene

the ethnographical level, they exceed the bounds of traditional social photography or political documentation. Following his long period of aestheticism and gentle lyricism, a vital stream of life, a spicy wind emanated from Luckus' photography. The photographer was attracted by vigorous people and dynamic situations, and most of all by the vitality of the world unleashing the indescribable freedom of existential and natural forms which might be conceived as disorder by some. No hierarchy of meaning exists in his multi-plane pictures: a place overgrown with nettles, a railway platform, a restaurant spoon, a propaganda poster and a man acting with childish seriousness are all equally important elements. The beautiful and the ugly are written down here in black on white – or in white on black? Truth in his concept of the world lies not beyond a transcendental horizon where analysing thought would drive it, but coincides completely with reality and reveals itself as an entirety to the profound and momentary vision. Luckus had no hesitation in stripping off the layers of words, ideas, ideologies, judgements and definitions to uncover fragmentary sparks of truth – naked existence.

The images and their meaning also cannot be separated because they are not split apart by the traditional compositional scheme. Luckus regarded conventional models of composition – invented and copied by others – as an obstacle on the road toward true realism. He therefore used to concentrate visual material in his own way. His motto was to destroy and annihilate the composition, and he pursued this aim with all his youthful passion. Through his initial conflict with the language of photography, he was able to penetrate deeply into its possibilities. Later on he made use of all these possibilities, beginning with the most mysterious ones.

Luckus used to say that professionalism, rules of composition and lighting, stereotypes of form, push aside certain elements without which the image of life lacks completeness. That is why he persistently strove to express the indivisibility of Man and his surroundings, the spontaneity of each situation. He had a particular flair for locating the most vital spots of reality, where healthy vigor creates forms of life beyond ideologies and theories. He intuitively grasped the phenomenological aspect of photographic expression and tried to formulate it in his diary:

'Photographs are no icons, and the women in them are no Marias or Magdalenas. They are the expression of real endless and infinite power. This must not be stereotyped by personal feelings or thoughts'.

While eliminating the classical structure of images, Luckus never aimed at originality of form, at blinding expressiveness for its own sake. He used to declare his aim as 'the actual vision' – the truth. By ruthlessly subordinating all aesthetic aspects to the expression of truth, he seemed provincially naive and old-fashioned – at least in the opinion of our most prominent aestheticians who raised an anti-gnoseologist rebellion a decade ago. Nevertheless, Luckus had a deep knowledge of modern art and the range of its problems. This makes his struggle for truth against the 'leaden veil' of formality (Luckus) even more significant.

The independent path chosen by Luckus is already apparent in his early works 'Pantomime' and 'Improvising Pantomime'. These freely utilize the entire arsenal of avant-garde photography without restriction (as the French art critic J.C. Lemagny once pointed out). Trying to penetrate the drama of human dualism and self-expression which is the main topic of these works, Luckus created a secondary reality. Here environment and space are entirely subdued to the expressionist revelation of mood as well as the feelings of depression, menace and restriction. On this photographic stage the human figures lose their individuality – so highly valued later – and become abstract hieroglyphs. The roots of this can be found both in the art of our century and in the natural ability of the subconscious to create chimerical visions with coded meanings.

The transformation from fragmentary to wholist thinking in the documentary makes every element of the image important. It leaves no room for photographic fortuities (which are the scourge of any documentary). This means the embryo of the image is formed not in the whirlpool of egocentric emotions, but by recognizing the superior status of reality – by joyfully discovering that the world is developing according to a much wiser plan than we could possibly devise. Here lies the source of enjoying all details the endless variety and perfect individuality of which far exceed the bounds of our imagination.

In order to describe the final stage of evolution in Luckus' understanding of photography, it is necessary to refer to his last work, never shown in any exhibition – his book 'Attitude toward Old Photography'. Having strived stubbornly for originality, Luckus used none of his own photographs in his last work. Rather like Thomas Stearns Eliot, creating freely from a treasury of globally accumulated images, Luckus freely chose and combined photographic images. Names, titles and text were excluded from the book lest they should interfere with these images and prevent them from uniting into an aggregate where the underlying formula of life – the DNA – regulates our spiritual nature.

The world in this book is tragic, full of destruction and suffering. Man is depicted as mixture of terrible vice and love. The author does not allow him to turn into a monster, however, plunging into the depths of senseless amidst these waves of destruction. Human hope makes the world seem beautiful to him. Rather than stoical, this hope is sooner naive, with a childish simplicity which continues until death. To look upon the world with such forgiving sadness and admiring surprise is only possible from a very great distance. From this range the world seems concentrated into an existential dot, a flying torpedo. Luckus uses its repeated image to incarnate the face of destiny. Beauty and rudeness, spirituality and materialism are stripped of the distinguishing features attributed to them by the language of words. We see now why Luckus valued the unique quality of photographic language so highly. Our understanding of his work is completed, however, by the following words from his diary:

'In the beginning I tried to classify my work according to social phenomena and photogaphical style, emphasizing the topic of life and death. This made me feel like a Lithuanian artist carving statues of God or the saints. When I put everything on the table, however, I felt like a god myself. In front of me I had an Asian and a Red Indian, a Negro, a white, a Moslem, a Buddhist, a Christian, the Czarist army, the Polish army, the Kaiser, the war, funerals and weddings. I shuffled thousands of images into a heap and found they were an orderly heap of life, because everything here was life and because all of us, whether a boxer, a Czar, a beggar or a half-naked woman were disclosed here. Archive photography seemed to me to reflect a bottomless well, waiting for somebody to look into it and understand it'.

After finishing this book, Luckus seemed to have exhausted all his photographic challenges, and his creative genius was firmly gripped by a desire to turn his darkroom into a carpenter's workshop as soon as possible. Pencil in hand, he drew sketches of the furniture he would make: sometimes baroque, sometimes– that of

Secession – a kind of eclectic mixture of stranger ideas and tastes. Rather than lifting a finger to acquire any carpenter's tools, however, he decided before leaving the darkroom to 'publish' at least four copies of the book all by himself.

In actual fact only two copies were printed – not books in the traditional sense. Since he had no hope of having his works published or displayed, Luckus compiled four books of documentary and portrait photography from original prints. One copy should have been deposited in the Photographers' Union library, so that at least his colleagues could see what he had done. The other was to be kept at home and shown to friends from Russia and the Ukraine who dropped in frequently.

Unfortunately Antanas Sutkus, President of the Photographers' Union at that time and a famous art photographer, refused to admit Luckus' books to the library or even place them on a shelf. Although he was used to such setbacks by then, this was quite a shock to the author. A conference of Union members was soon to take place, so he desperately declared that he would publicly donate the books to the library at this conference so that no one would dare turn down such a present. Nevertheless, after receiving several pleas not to get the organization into trouble, he rejected the idea. From then on, his powerful and vital nature started to lose its vigor. His suicide a few years later came as no surprise to the photographic world.

Luckus had an excellent understanding of the singularity and value of what he had done, and thought he had the right to claim other people's attention. His powerful, spontaneous and independence-seeking personality did not free him from the natural desire of every artist to live to see himself recognized.

On the contrary, one of his greatest passions was to enter into a true dialogue with the world, and many of his works were secretly intended to provoke this dialogue. Sadly, the impervious but cunning political system at that time had hundreds of ways of putting creative individuals into isolation.

It would be erroneous to picture Luckus as a traditional rebel against the political system and the Soviet regime, however. His works have political implications inasmuch as they reveal the truth of life, in which politics is only one of many aspects. His confrontation with the political system occurred solely because there was no room for his work in the field of established possibilities – the official territory of the beautiful.

Luckus' spirit raged, failing to find enough room in the paradigm of politics and the 'normal life'. The actual cause of his youthful rebellion was the shallowness of most human conventions, both in relationships and artistic tastes. Somewhat later came a bitter awareness of existential boundaries, the illegibility of the world, the inadequacy of human oral and artistic speech to express his intuitions, and the resulting deformed communication and estrangement. He had numerous connections – both normal and highly unusual – with people of various nationalities and professions. Among these poets, drivers, drunkards, priests, he continuously searched for a dialogue partner. All the Russian verses and drunken brawls were intended to provoke such a dialogue – not on what was happening in the world, but on its sense.

Nocturnal pub-crawls round Vilnius with Muscovite friends or his dog Simba were the sort of events which made a bad impression on decent citizens. Having woken up some acquaintances at midnight, he would ask for a newspaper and then lie down on it with Simba in the kitchen. *'I'm a mongrel'*, he would say after sobering up. And *'Mongrel Luckus'* is how he signed his Christmas cards. In this half-joking manner he tried to learn how to be a nobody in society. Nevertheless, the tragic end to his life showed that he never succeeded. He was too proud – in the same way as Shakespeare who is said to have introduced himself to the Queen as the 'king of words'. Luckus, who often mentioned this anecdote, probably felt he was mastering the language of photography more and more perfectly.

In fact he regarded photography as a laconic language for communicating many things simultaneously. In order to say everything he wanted, he aimed to master it perfectly. This slightly childish but indescribably strong compulsion gave him the energy for experimentation, for stubbornly purifying the photographic language.

After ascending to the heights of his style, however, he suddenly had a revelation while working on 'Attitude toward Old Photography'. The world seemed to open up and speak to him without a medium; it was speech itself. A primitive photo postcard, or the Baltic wind shaking petals and blowing sweepings around Vilnius railway station, says a lot to those who can listen. This was a shock to Luckus. It was not he who had something to say to the world – he merely had to listen, and his purified language was only necessary for asking his questions correctly.

I happened to be a witness of his last plans and insights. We used to talk through the library window because Luckus would not come into the room – the conversation might then seem too traditionally serious. He fired off his conclusions hastily and with a smile, looking around nervously to see if he was believed. Afterwards he would quickly retire in order not hear any counter-arguments, comparisons with Eastern philosophy or the like.

From his point of view, he was expressing his individual, unique experience, his own discovery.

Left without its usual occupation, however, the other side of his personality began to deteriorate rapidly. He drank too much, and often became aggressive. It only needed the jeer of a colleague at his work to provoke the tragic end.

When all is said and done, Luckus completed his difficult quest – the search for truth and sense – victoriously and not as a victim. Images of a strong and healthy life designed into perfect compositions still bespeak his initial joy in the beauty of life and his reflecting soul.

Biography 1943 **born 29 May in Kaunas, Lithuania. Father a carpenter and wood engraver.** 1950-1961 secondary education in an

art college where also he learns painting. 1955 his parents offer him his first camera, an Agfa. 1956 begins his 'Relatives' series

(continuing). 1958 develops great interest in art photography. 1960 joins Kaunas Photo Club. 1961 starts working on the 'Collea-

gues' series. 1962 **elected as president of Kaunas Photo Club.** 1965-1967 military service. 1967 settles in Vilnius. Studies colour

photography independently. Begins to work in advertising photography. First publication of his work. 1967-1971 b & w 'Mimme'

series about the drama in human life. 1969-1975 produces series of documentaries in Georgia, Russia, Armenia in which he stres-

ses human psychology, the social environment, the spontaneity of life. Photojournalist, documentary reportages for the magazi-

nes Švyturys, Tarybine moteris, Buitis, Kinas, Šeima, Soviet Life, Sovetskij Sojuz, and the newspaper Czerwony Sztandar. Illustra-

tes many magazine covers. Photographer for the Banga fashion magazine. 1969 **marries Tanya Luckiene.** 1969-1987 works on the

series of 'Close-ups'. 1970-1973 photographs and prepares book on the Kaunas pantomime troupe. 1974 begins the 'Attitude

towards Old Photography' series with his collection of old photographs. Makes montages of these images, incorporating his own

photographs. 1975 starts also 'Emotions' series. 1976 resumes advertising photography. Works for Intourist agency Moscow.

Designer in Moscow for the National Achievements (national and international exhibitions). 1982 prepares a retrospective with

500 photographs. 1983 transforms his 'Pantomime' images using montage and serigraphy techniques. 1983 Interview with And-

reij Speranskij. 1985 **Exhibition in the palace of artists, Vilnius.** 1986 **Exhibition in Tallin.** 1986-1987 Prints and makes originals of

5 different photo-albums, each in two copies: 1 Impressions; 2 Relatives and Colleagues; 3 Azerbaijan, Bashkiria; 4 Estonia, Geor-

gia, Alta; 5 Attitudes towards Old Photography. In this album he uses old photographs and makes collages with these.

1987 Starts a new cyclus; 'On a white background', people on the market.

Exhibitions 1982 **Creative Photo Camp, Nida, Retrospective; Art Research Institute, Moscow; Stroganov Art Institute, Moscow;**

Sovietskij Sojuz, Moscow; Studencheskij meridian, Moscow; Technicheskaya aestetika, Moscow; Kiev University, Kiev; Residence

of APN, Kiev; La Photographie Lituanienne, Centre de la Photographie, Genève.

1986 the Pushkin Museum buys 29 works by Luckus.

Bibliography 1967 Lietuvos fotografija; 1969 **Sovetskoje foto no. 10, Lietuvos fotografija;** 1970 **Sovetskoje foto no. 3 & no. 11;**

1971 **Fotografija no. 8 & no. 12, Lietuvos fotografija;** 1972 **Noorus no. 7;** 1974 Lietuvos fotografija; 1978,1981 Lietuvos fotografi-

ja; 1982 **Studencheskij meridian no. 7 & no. 8.** 1983 Interpressgrafic (H), Interpressgrafic (SU), Fotografie revue (CS)

Biography

Vitas Luckus

Photographs

Friends and Relatives

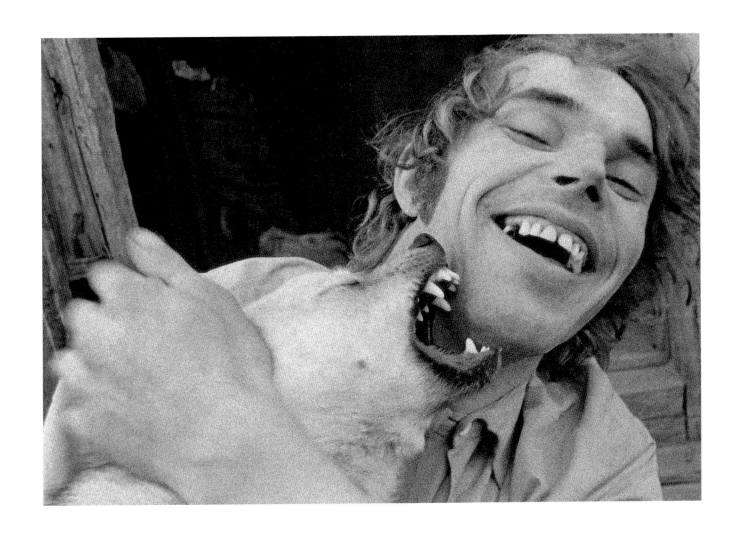

Journeys to Azerbaijan, Bashkiria

Journeys to Estonia, Georgia, Alta

Impressions

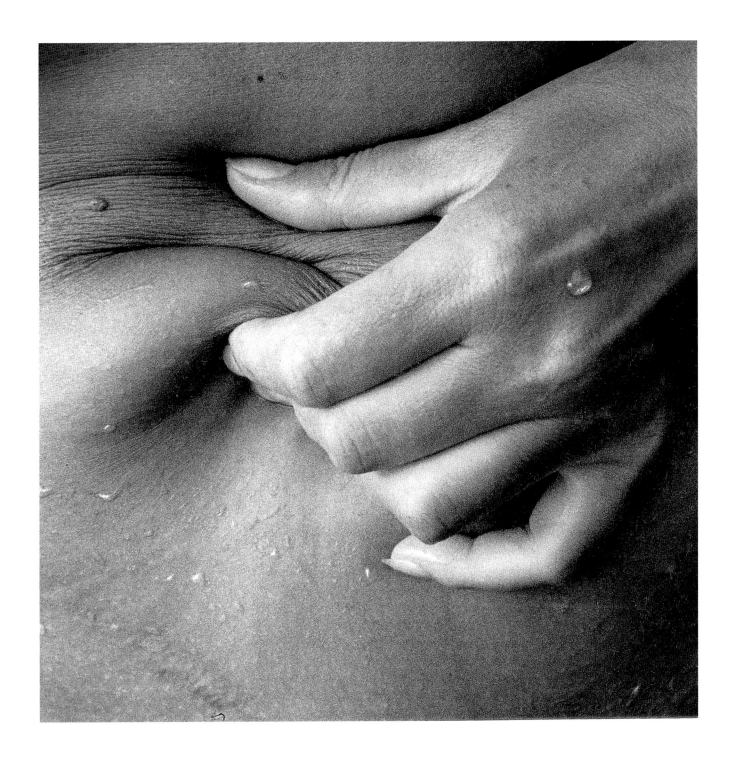

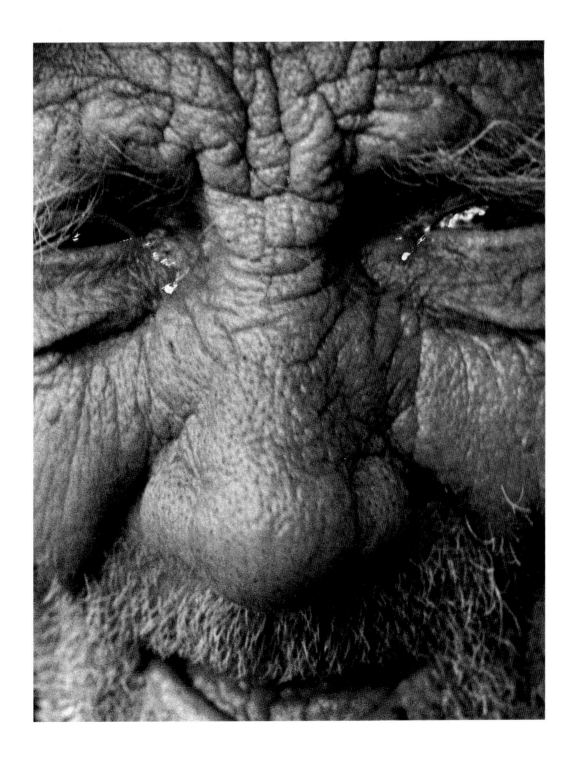

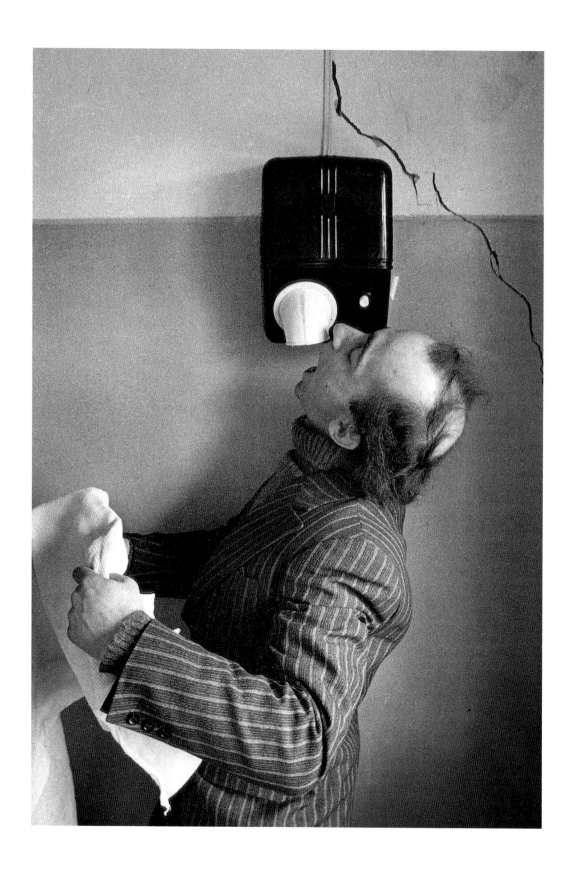

100

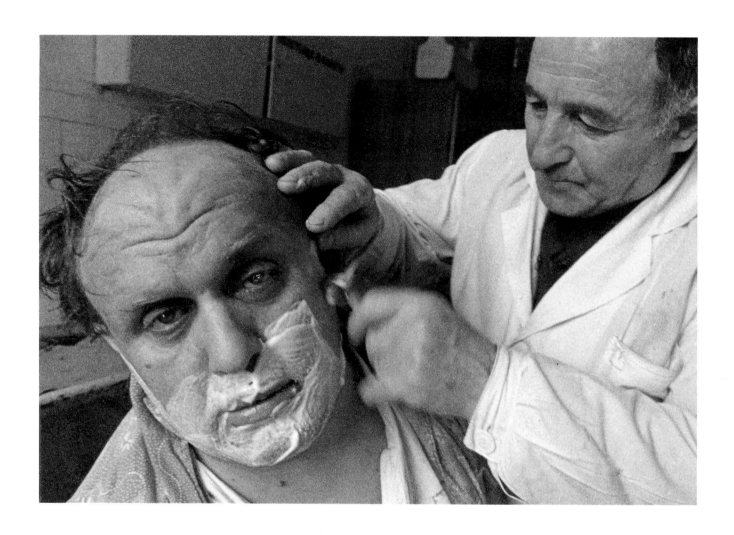

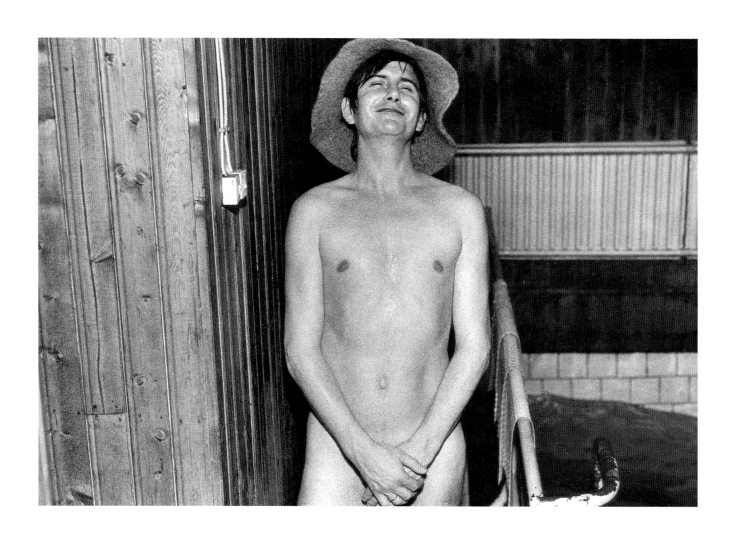

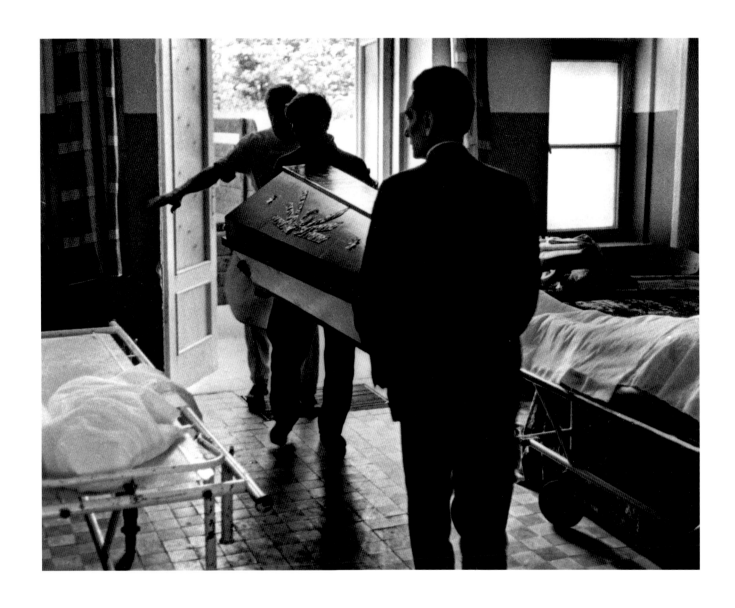

On the south-eastern edge of Vilnius, where the motorways to Lida and Minsk leave the city, there is a hill with a small cemetery. It is not difficult to imagine why people selected this spot to bury their dead. From the slope of the hill where the graves are dug, the view extends across the valley down to Vilnius. It is a peaceful scene, although modern times have disfigured it with wide strips of asphalt, like runways issuing from the foot of the hillside cemetery. Regarded as an obstacle by engineers and roadbuilders at the time, it was only with the greatest of efforts that people managed to prevent the entire hill from being removed. And still there are fears that eventually the cemetery will succumb to the pressure of progress. The almost shameless construction of the motorway, to which part of the hill has already been sacrificed, coincides with the rhythm of change in Lithuania. Vitas Luckus would not have allowed himself to be troubled by it.

More than anyone else, Luckus knew that life held no promise whatsoever, not even after death, and that it only exists by virtue of the illusion that it will continue. His grave is austere.
It consists of a frame of blue marble bands, enclosing the stubborn soil, the unyielding reddish brown. Something actually grows in this unlikely place. The rising green must be of a strong species. Luckus lies next to his mother's grave; his daughter, Matija Vito Luckute, who did not survive her birth in May 1984, is buried further up the hill. It is a mournful place where much grief has been gathered.

'There is still a lot to be done.' Not long before his death, Luckus wrote this phrase on the door of the basement which served as his darkroom and studio. It can be interpreted in different ways, depending on intonation. Perhaps it refers to a task which concerns the whole world, but Luckus may just as well have intended it as a statement about his own life.
Vitas Luckus was an impassioned spirit. The will to register the world in creative photography prevailed over his occasional feelings of impotence. In a way, his appeal for action, *'There is still a lot to be done,'* can be

The Hard Way [1]

Herman Hoeneveld

taken as a warning; an ominous signal foreshadowing his death. He had threatened to commit suicide on one occasion, and once actually made an abortive suicide attempt. To his wife and his friends, both the threat and the attempt signified no more than lugubrious but characteristic jokes rather than serious attempts to leave the world. There is no doubt that he realized the hook on which he had fixed the rope would never have been able to withstand his weight.

Vitas Luckus' life was largely dominated by an almost obsessional desire to grasp the essence of life itself by means of photography, images and even words. Luckus also wanted to be a poet, and he wrote many impassioned letters particularly during the sixties and seventies. They centre around the themes of life and death, love and alcohol as frequently as his photographs.

Vitas Luckus was born in the city of Kaunas on 29 May 1943[2]. At the age of eighteen he concluded a secondary art course, graduating in drawing and painting. In the meantime, an Agfa presented to him by his parents had roused his interest in photography. In 1962 he became chairman of the local photographic society, in which so-called art photographers organized themselves according to the model prescribed by the authorities, as usual in the former Soviet Union.[3]

Five years later, he moved to Vilnius[4] and contributed to the foundation of the Photography Art Society of Lithuania, which later was to be changed and expanded, and renamed the Photography Union of Lithuania.[5] In 1969 he married Tanya Luckiene. During the period between 1969 and 1975 he made a name for himself as a press photographer for the Lithuanian media. From 1975 onwards he worked as a free-lance photographer. Although friends and enemies alike acknowledged his talent, his qualities were almost completely ignored by the authoities. This must have contributed significantly to his growing sense of frustration and bitterness, which eventually ended in the catastrophe of 16 March 1987, including murder and suicide.

After numerous conversations with his wife Tanya, his friends, colleagues, acquaintances as well as outsiders, I was left with a confused image of Vitas Luckus. Fortunately, his photographs create a different impression. They speak for themselves and particularly reveal Luckus' keen eye and sympathy for the uniqueness of human beings and their craving for freedom.

It would be too easy to interpret Luckus' rebellious and occasionally provocative behaviour as outbursts of pent-up frustration with the regime. The boundless energy that was in him not only benefited his work. Many people were inspired by the intensity of his spirit, both in his direct environment and in other circles where his name was known. His house was a meeting place for artists and close friends. He had a unique inspiring and stimulating effect on others, and could work for days on end with a minimum of sleep and alcohol (vodka). To be sure, his stamina, which has become legendary by now, not only expressed itself in working but also, and emphatically, in drinking. Even when it seems obvious that alcohol contributes to relaxation almost everywhere in the world, although some find it difficult to moderate themselves, the former Soviet Union, rather than confirming this rule, appears to be an exception, Without exaggeration, drinking in this part of the world is best described as alcohol abuse on a grand scale. More recently, some traditional explanations for this, such as the characteristically long and severe winters or the eternal poverty of the Soviet people, were joined by new incentives for a collective refuge in alcohol: frustration after the ideal communist state failed to materialize, the virtual absence of an alternative to vodka, and the benefits which the authorities derived from preserving the permanent intoxication of a half-drunk nation – all these factors contributed to excessive alcohol consumption by the Soviet people.

In the early seventies, Vitas Luckus began to work in cooperation with a man called Šarunas Davainis.[6] They initiated a 'prize' production project. These prizes were sold at collective farms and factories, where outstanding workers were awarded trophies (obviously as an alternative to pay rises). Davainis, who was already involved in the amber trade at the time (and since then has developed an impressive enterprise in this sector), proved to be the ideal complement to Luckus' talent. Every time Luckus launched a new idea, Davainis managed to provide the technical and organizational support required for its realization. Davainis soon became head of Luckus' studio and darkroom facilities. Together they developed and produced all kinds of practical solutions and applications, which gave Luckus' photography studio a considerable lead in the field. They were commissioned, for example, to produce large light boxes for slides, and made a good profit on them. On another occasion they were asked to design the interior of a restaurant in a provincial town. They used the considerable profit made on that order to buy a house in the neighbourhood and, like mischievous schoolboys, decided to celebrate their success with a vodka drinking competition in their new abode. When, after a few hours, they had exhausted their supply, they drove to a nearby village, bought fresh bottles and continued their binge until eventually they dropped down unconscious. The next morning they were 'clinically dead', to use Davainis' own words. However, they were both physically strong enough to prevent a real and premature death. Once they had more or less regained consciousness, the question who had won remained to be answered. Having been sufficiently sober to drive a car, Luckus proclaimed himself the winner of the vodka contest. Looking back on this anecdote and other, similar events in the past, Davainis agrees that Vitas drank far too heavily, but adds that he was not the only one. Living in a grey area between reality and fantasy, daily life compelled people to seek refuge in alcohol. Davainis is convinced that Vitas Luckus was very much aware of this process.

Antanas Sutkus, co-founder and chairman of the Photography Art Society Lithuania, was a friend and colleague of Vitas Luckus for a number of years. In addition to his widespread reputation as a photographer, Sutkus was known to be a heavy drinker. Sutkus' daily work frequently made him associate with Russian officials or Lithuanian authorities. He still regards drinking as the 'state language' in which people communicated in those circles. Not being a member of the Communist Party could, under certain conditions, be forgiven, but abstaining from alcohol simply turned a person into a nonentity. Sutkus remembers all too well the early years of his acquaintance with Luckus. To stress the extent of their drinking, he points out that he has never been able to determine who was the heavier drinker: Luckus or he himself. In his account, Sutkus complains that while he had to drag himself to the offices of the photography society day in day out, Vitas could stay in bed to sleep off his hangover.

Particularly during the early years of his career, Luckus' heavy drinking, preferably in the company of one or two friends, seems to have been a game rather than inevitable escapism. In addition to being a (male) cultural phenomenon, alcohol abuse became a means of expression. Social control was different from what we mean by it in the West, and did little to prevent drunkenness, if anything at all. On the contrary, feelings released by alcohol were felt to merit a certain positive approach. It was even better if you could share them and observe them in others. However, in certain circles and particularly in the Baltic republics there were people who refused to join in this more or less collective drinking habit. In many cases, these people were the ones who realized that vodka was being used as a panacea ruling the lives of an increasing number of people. Moreover, some people witnessed others becoming so dependent on alcohol as to lose all defence against the many-branched informer network operated by the KGB.

For many years vodka proved to be the best antidepressant, because it was the only one. Seminas Finkelšteinas[7] remembers all too well how twenty-year-old Vitas Luckus was introduced to the kind of drinking that was customary in those days. Luckus had confided to him that he had felt sorry for everything he had lost by not having started drinking earlier! It was only later (they continued to be friends even though they saw less of each other than they used to) that Finkelšteinas realized how well the alcohol abuse of some could serve others. At the Photography Art Society office, for instance, Vitas Luckus could easily be branded as a drinking dissident, so as to discredit his personality and render his position untenable. Vitas Luckus frequently consumed more vodka than most others could possibly handle. However, Sutkus is not the only one to confirm that, in spite of all this, Luckus was never regarded as an alcoholic. It would seem more accurate to associate his excessive drinking with a lack of real friends, who might have enabled him to unleash his energy in a different way than with vodka. Time and again, both his friends and enemies were amazed at the passion with which he threw himself into his work and ideas. The role of alcohol was no different in his life than in the life of the average Soviet citizen, although the extent to which he indulged in it was staggering, and worried many people around him. Not least his wife Tanya, who, like so many other women in the former Soviet Union, eventually resigned herself to it.

A gifted person does not consist of harmonious components only. Contradictions and mutually exclusive traits typically characterize brilliant and creative spirits. Many people took the darker side of Vitas Luckus' personality for granted. Richardas Niuniavas[8] cooperated with him for many years. Like a brother and a teacher, Luckus helped his younger cousin in his struggle through adolescence. Richardas passed his driving test, travelled with Luckus to Azerbaijan and Georgia, and gradually became his partner. As time went on he identified with his master to such an extent that, according to his acquaintances, he actually began to copy his traits. Something similar happened to another assistant, Vytas Janulis, and it seems obvious that the example held up by Luckus greatly inspired various people. His unpredictable behaviour endeared him to some, while others strongly envied, if not hated, him for it. He could be unexpectedly and overwhelmingly charming, and when in love he would buy flowers and present them in public to the person to whom he had lost his heart, for as long as it lasted. With a similar kind of impetuosity he could share a success with others, for instance by throwing a party in some restaurant for no apparent reason. In the intensity of his emotions he sometimes seemed to lose his sense of proportions, although it may just as well be his sense of theatre and spectacle that is still haunting

Richardas' thoughts. Others, too, cherish intense memories of Luckus, as an outspoken personality which distinguished itself from his more timid fellow human beings.

In the early eighties, Luckus managed to travel to Prague. More or less kindred spirits there succeeded in publishing photographs by Luckus in a magazine. When this publication later caught the eye of the authorities, Luckus was plainly given to understand that it had virtually ruined his opportunities as a photographer. It was one of his many collisions with the regime.

Milda Šeškuviene[9] points out the contradictions in his character, which seemed to find expression even in his movements. His mood could radically change from one moment to the other, often as a result of some remark about his work. Yet she did not leave the impression that Luckus was an insecure person who could not bear any criticism. As time went on, Luckus had enough reason to doubt the sincerity of other people's judgement. It became increasingly clear to him that, from a distance and via obscure methods, attempts were being made to boycott his work. In 1982, Milda S. made a TV programme about him. Realizing the significance of half an hour's TV coverage, Luckus was absorbed in preparations for an entire week prior to the planned broadcast. Even though Milda remembers him as being extremely tense during this period, the shooting went fine and everybody was more than satisfied. The tremendous disillusion following the censor's order to cut the whole programme was one of the many blows Luckus suffered. In 1986, there was an unexpected opportunity to stage an exhibition at the official Vilnius artists' centre. The chairman of the Photographic Art Society, who had allowed himself to be shaped into a boycott instrument for the KGB's private use, happened to be on holiday. Milda S. convinced Luckus of the fact that now the opportunity had come to exhibit his work, and take revenge at the same time. However, the fear that, yet again, this event was going to be cancelled at the last moment so obsessed him, that he spoilt this opportunity by indulging in excessive drinking just when the show was about to be staged. In the summer of the same year, during the annual seminar[10], Luckus caused a great commotion with his presentation of no less than 500 photographs, all in passe-partout. This extravagant call for recognition was acknowledged and, in a way, also accepted. Many felt ashamed about the performance of their chairman on the one hand, and about their failure to rise against it on the other. Change may have been in the air even then, but no substantial improvement in the freedom of mind and action had as yet been introduced. For Luckus, the most significant step forward was his appointment to the organisation's art council. This council provided advice on artistic policy, assessed the work of candidate-members, made proposals for presentations, exhibitions and publications and recommended members and works for representation abroad.

'Strong as a horse': this is how Grigori Kanovich[11] summarizes his vague recollections of Vitas Luckus. He was a strange person, yet human. He photographed both for God and for the devil, and worked as if possessed. Kanovich once learnt that Luckus also wanted to write. To express his view of life even better, even more poignantly? Luckus himself sanctioned this suspicion by saying, *'The world of thoughts and feelings fits in 3 x 4 cm as well as in metres of canvas. The main thing is that our souls shouldn't just stay on paper but strike root in life.'* He was haunted by the urge to do more, to accomplish still more in life. He was fascinated by travelling and attracted to the unknown. In other countries he met people who seemed to live like nomads like himself, almost independently from political systems. Kanovich describes Luckus' urge to travel as the passion of a person yearning to shed his skin, feeling imprisoned in his body. The author imagines that it was these feelings of restlessness that caused Luckus' strong and occasionally unpleasant emotions. Socially, Luckus was brilliant at certain moments, impossible at others. He did not really fit in his environment; he generally lacked the skill of getting along with people, and functioned better when alone. Perhaps this is why he sometimes preferred the company of animals to that of people, such as his dog Simba or the young lion which he took as a pet, to the dismay of many.

He was equally fitful in his relationships with women. However, shallow women without brains or personality never held his attention for long, if at all. Insiders have pointed out that, while suffering from his escapades, his wife never left him, even though life with him must have been unbearable during certain periods. Luckus' jealousy was easy to provoke and uncommonly fierce, and he proved to be a poor judge of the ordinary and well-intentioned attention which friends displayed towards his wife.

In letters which Luckus wrote to his wife, Tanya Luckiene, while he was doing his military service and when travelling, he touched upon the subject of suicide a number of times, as a solution to his despair at the decline of their love which he imagined to be taking place. He expressed the threat in passionate terms, referring to earlier declarations and resolutions. In some passages the echoes of a fierce argument still reverberate.

'I wrote a letter yesterday, posted it, and this one I'll write now and post it too, because I can't bear that everything is so silly, so ridiculous, and yet so powerful, so wonderful and simple. Earlier I wanted to commit suicide. I wanted it all the time. Today I want purity, dreams and happiness.'

And a bit further in the same letter:

'We have to give all for the greater good, maybe I'm saying this because I myself am terrified. I want, perhaps, to persuade myself that I'm seriously ill so that it is not a shame to die. Distance, the fact that you are somewhere far away, doesn't confuse me. It is clear to me. I love you ... I pray to God to take us into his care. We have to solve a lot of problems, don't we?'

In a different letter, written in a strange key, he describes how he was thrown off balance by his wife's absence and vainly tried to travel to her. He failed to catch a train or aeroplane, and begged her to write or call him.

'Write me, please, about how you like the trip. I'll hang myself otherwise before you're back. Vitas.'

While travelling himself, and describing his feelings about the approaching birth of their child, he refers to the continuous strain that characterized their relationship.

'As far as the baby is concerned, I want a baby and I want him to be mine. Maybe my wishes will come true? We should never quarrel again. I will love and respect you. Oh, I am stupid. How I hurt you; but I promise it won't happen again, in the name of our love and real friendship. If there's no real love, then to the devil with everything ...'

The conflict that marred their relationship urged him to thorough self-reflection, at least in his letters.

'When I'm back with Simba [his dog] he runs all over the place searching and then, finding nothing, he comes to me and looks. I sit down on the sea chest, [a piece of furniture they kept shoes in] pat him and then I understand what's wrong: Tanya isn't there. She isn't there! O, I don't care to think that there's a gulf between us. The only gulf is alcohol. I don't think I am an alcoholic, only it is hard to resist it. We would be much happier without it. Please, I beg you, help me. I agree that it isn't going to be easy, but I believe it is possible. We have three options: divorce, living together while being indifferent to each other, or loving each other in full trust and harmony. I choose the third one. We should destroy all that was bad in the past and leave only the good memories and wonderful future perspectives. Everything depends on us and I trust our wisdom. If we lose this chance now, I fear that tomorrow will be too late. We may not find anything in our separate new lives. And our memories will torture us. Our destiny is in our hands; we shouldn't cast our fate to the winds.'

P.S. Simba is lying on the armchair and doesn't care, or at least he pretends not to. I am waiting for you, Vitas.'

'A tragic event occurred on 16 March, 1987.[12] It destroyed our family and changed my life forever. On that day, some people came to our flat. They said that they were guests, but personally I never invited anybody. Still, Vitas received them. To me, most of them were complete strangers. They looked at books and photographs made by Luckus. One of these people, named *Krakauskas*, mocked and ridiculed my husband, abusing him and his work and continuously insinuating something which apparently only my husband was able to understand. I noticed that Vitas was nervous and upset. He kept silent and looked at this man with a strange expression in his eyes. He also looked desperate. I did not understand what was going on. When I went to the kitchen to prepare some food, I heard screams in the room. I ran back and saw Krakauskas lying on the floor, stabbed. The others left immediately. I wanted to call an ambulance but I just could not bring myself to speak. My husband called the ambulance himself. When the medical team arrived, they told me that Krakauskas was dead. It was Vitas who had stabbed him. I went to look for him in the study. I entered the room and saw the window open. I went to the balcony and looking down I saw my husband lying in the yard. I was shocked. I went downstairs, without saying a word to the ambulance team. Vitas was still warm, but I realized that he was dead. I lay down beside him in the snow, motionless. I do not remember the rest. The ambulance team took me back to the flat where they gave me some medication. Among them was Leonid, the KGB man who had been appointed to look after Vitas during 'perestroika'.

A week later, the official announcement of Vitas' death was published. It was discussed in the highest circles of the government, for Vitas had been one of Lithuania's leading photographers. After nine more days I was invited to the prosecutor's office, where I was told that the case had already been closed. I was shown pictures of the bodies and that was it. No matter how hard I tried to extract information from them about what had happened and who this Krakauskas was, they kept silent and refused to answer my questions. Later, I was informed by friends that Krakauskas had been a KGB agent.'

The macabre role played by the KGB in Vitas Luckus' life began when he was doing his military service. One day Luckus was asked by an officer to decorate the reception area of his barracks with photographs, on the occasion of a high military visit. In compensation, Luckus was promised ten days' leave in order to go to Moscow, where his work was being exhibited. However, he was only granted three days instead of ten. He did travel to Moscow all the same and, of course, outstayed his leave. On his return he was seized by panic when he was spotted by a military patrol. In his attempt to flee, he was run over by a trolley bus and broke his leg. He was put in prison, asked for medical aid but was deliberately ignored. After a long time, a KGB agent appeared who said he wanted to help him. He accepted the offer, for which he was to pay for the rest of his life, because the KGB wanted his cooperation. Tanya Luckiene described their life under the permanent terror of threat and blackmail by the secret service as a nightmare.

The KGB wanted Luckus to cooperate in the 'usual' way: to pass on what he knew about foreigners and to provide confidential information about his friends. Initially, when he categorically refused to cooperate, Luckus was given to understand that each refusal would result in an extra six months of military service. They would not hesitate to arrest him in his bed if necessary. Many years of torment and intimidation were to follow. Luckus was frequently forced to report to the KGB, where he was told there was no way out and that it would be wiser to cooperate. Various incidents then punctuated the bizarre route followed by the KGB to increase pressure on him. In 1976 their flat was burgled. KGB agents stole a huge collection of negatives which Luckus had made before and during his military service. He was beaten up several times, in the street, in toilets at restaurants and cafes. When his wife asked him what had happened he would only give a vague answer. Only after disconnecting the phone would he tell her that he had been arrested in the street, taken away and cross-examined. The burglaries were repeated, evidently intended to intimidate them. A few times KGB agents called on him at home. On these occasions, Vitas asked his wife to stay away for a couple of hours, frightened as he was that they would hurt her too.

In 1981, he and his wife visited an exhibition of his work in Moscow which had been sharply criticized by the authorities. After the visit, they were invited to a Finnish sauna by people they did not know. An officer who 'happened' to be present at the sauna told Vitas casually that he might slip and end up on the scalding hot stones below. Luckus tried hard to keep the grim grip of the KGB on his life hidden from others. In 1985 the pressure was further increased. Another agent, called Leonid, came on the scene. When they moved to another flat their telephone appeared to be out of order. It was not until some time had passed when a repairman turned up, who quickly stated that he could not solve the problem. The next day, somebody else came to fiddle with the telephone. He got it to work again. From then on, their conversations were monitored.

The KGB terrorized people's daily lives. At parties, any discussion on politics was avoided, since there was always the danger that one of your friends or acquaintances was part of the KGB network. Not even relatives could be trusted. As a friend and a colleague, Šarunas Davainis was aware of Vitas' assumption that the KGB were trying to use him. All the same, Davainis still wonders what reason the KGB might have had for making life so difficult for a person like Vitas. However, he confirms that the KGB frequently adopted these tactics to recruit informants. He himself had been asked to cooperate at the age of fourteen.

Others, too, are still not sure whether Vitas Luckus' suicide was an incident provoked by the KGB or a coincidence of completely uncontrolled emotions, tragic but no less predictable, and excessive drinking, heavy strain and injured pride.

The few things we know about what really happened on that fatal night at least allow us to confirm that Krakauskas made highly derogatory remarks about Luckus' work. With the obvious purpose of provoking Luckus' anger, Krakauskas openly wondered why his work should cause such a fuss. (On the previous day an exhibition had been opened with work from some one hundred photographers, at which Luckus, for the first time in his life, was amply and respectfully represented, one wall being devoted to portraits of his hand. His insecurity and pent-up frustrations had led him to attract attention to himself by wondering whether he was going to be the only one to get TV coverage). Krakauskas went out of his way to revive the humiliations which Luckus had suffered in the past. Moreover, the police report is said to have made reference to extremely rude remarks in Russian on the part of Krakauskas, dirty insinuations intended to create the impression that he had had an affair with Luckus' wife.

One of the most depressing pieces of evidence about the far-reaching influence of the KGB is presented by the man who for many years, in his capacity as chairman of the Lithuanian Photographic Society, systematically cooperated in the boycott of Vitas Luckus. Antanas Sutkus refers to Vitas Luckus, of all people, as the only friend he has ever had: a posthumous Judas kiss. According to Sutkus, his good personal contacts with the KGB might have produced an arrangement in which Luckus would be declared to be of unsound mind, and be sent to a psychiatric asylum for three years at most.

Friends of Luckus believe that he preferred suicide when he realized what was going to come. Rather than prolonged agony with interrogations, solitary confinement, torture – rather than lifelong imprisonment that was to end in death anyway, he chose to rush to the end.

1 The text 'Vitas Luckus – The Hard Way' was written partly on the basis of conversations conducted in Lithuania with relatives, colleagues, friends and acquaintances of Vitas Luckus. With special thanks to Tanya Luckiene and many others, including Audra Baranauskaite; Šarunas Davainis; Semionas Finkelšteinas; Saule Gaizauskaite; Milda Šeškuviene; Grigori Kanovich; Ruta Kniukstiene; Lyalya Kuznetsova; Richardas Niuniava; Laima Skeiviene; Antanas Sutkus.

2 Kaunas is the second largest city in Lithuania, situated 95 km west of Vilnius. The city has appr. 430,000 inhabitants. When the Poles occupied parts of Lithuania in 1920, including Vilnius, Kaunas was proclaimed provisional capital of the independent republic. It retained this status until 1940, when the Second World War decided the fate of Lithuania, incorporating the republic in the USSR.

3 Like various other groups in the USSR (writers, artists), photographers were organized in an official union. This means that press photographers could join the Union of Press Photographers. These state-supervised organizations were spoon-fed by the authorities, who granted various privileges to their members. Those who did not join the unions were left without any opportunities to publish their work, stage exhibitions or maintain contacts abroad.

4 Vilnius, with almost 700,000 inhabitants, is the capital of Lithuania. Apart from its administrative function, Vilnius is the centre of the country from many other points of view as well. The city is situated at some thirty kilometres from the Byelorussian border.

5 Co-founded by the photographer Antanas Sutkus, one-time friend of Vitas Luckus and succeeded in 1990 by art historian Laima Skeiviene, joint author of this book.

6 At present, Šarunas Davainis is a successful businessman. He founded a company that deals in amber and which is now flourishing. In addition, he has been involved in politics since 1993.

7 Seminas Finkelšteinas is the marketing director of a technological research company in Vilnius. He and Luckus met when they were eighteen. Finkelšteinas used to be actively engaged in sports. Another visiting card says that 'Shimon Finkelstein' is presently active as chairman of the Lithuanian-Jewish sports club 'Maccabi'. In Lithuania it is the custom to adapt all names to the Lithuanian language.

8 Richardas Niuniavas is a cousin of Tanya Luckiene. In 1976, at the age of fifteen, he met Vitas Luckus and began to work for him in the darkroom, initially only on Sundays. He remained Luckus' assistant until 1985.

9 Milda Šeškuviene worked at the office of the photography society at the time, and knew Vitas Luckus well.

10 Each year, in the village of Nida on the Neringa peninsula, members of the photography society used to gather for a huge and largely informal meeting including lectures, presentations, portfolio reviews and discussions.

11 Grigori Kanovich (Kanovicius) is a Lithuanian-Jewish author, who was forced to write and publish in Russian. His works have been translated into other languages, however. Kanovich recently emigrated to Israel.

12 In 1991, after having emigrated to the United States, Luckus' widow Tanya Luckiene had an official statement drawn up about the death of her husband. This is a fragment from this statement.

The Chapter 'Friends and Relatives' features some colleagues of Vitas Luckus.

Page 26: A.Sliusarevas; page 27: S.Sgibnevas; page 28: B.Smelovas; page 29: A.Sapronenkovas; page 30: B.Smelovas, A.Sapronenkovas; page 33: A.Sutkaus Mamos Laidotuvés; page 34: B.Smelovas; page 35: B.Michailovas; page 36: B.Michailovas; page 37: A.Vartanovas; page 38: O.Polisčiukas; page 39: V.Arutiunovas, L.Silkinas; page 40: O.Polisčiukas; page 41: A.Speranskis, V.Koreškovas; page 42: V.Teresčenko, V.Arutiunovas; page 44-45: A.Sutkus.

Epilogue

To a considerable extent, the realization of this book was made possible thanks to the trust which Tanya Luckiene has placed in it. She was approached by publishers both from the West and from the former Soviet Union immediately after her husband's death. The idea to stage an exhibition and to make a book originated in August 1990, when I met Tanya Luckiene and was introduced to her husband's work. For her and her daughter the departure from Lithuania, leaving behind family and friends, signified a decisive deed leading to an utterly insecure future. In spite of all these radical changes, cares and almost constant strain she never lost her faith in the realization of the book and the exhibition. This faith was obviously reinforced when Cees de Jong of V+K Publishing and Thomas Stemmle of Edition Stemmle took the idea to heart. Perhaps one day another dream, to publish one of the books Luckus made himself, will also come true. An impressive and moving book, based on the images he came across in the course of his life, and with which he tells the story of mankind. There is still a lot to be done.

Herman Hoeneveld